Owned

One Handed Reads
Book 2

Dee Lish

'A truly submissive woman is to be treasured, cherished and protected for it is only she who can give a man the gift of dominance.'
    - Anne Desclos

Prologue

I had never really seen myself as a submissive. Quite the opposite, in fact. I was always dominating situations I was in, including sexually. Even if I was the subservient in the relationship, I still schemed, pushed, and 'topped from the bottom.' But my world fell apart when my partner took off with his secretary. I decided it was time for some changes. Time for some fun. That's how I met Owen.

I've known Owen for about five years now. I met him when I went to play some pool at the local university's bar with a few of the students I worked with. Owen was in his twenties, from Wales, and a student at the same university. I was in my early thirties. We flirted, we teased each other. We even had a very short period of dating, but in the end, we became best friends. I never would have dreamed it would turn out to be a lot more than that. My hot Welsh friend had a secret I didn't find out for a few years. He was a dominant: a Dom, a Master, a Sir.

At first, I thought nothing of it. I knew I wasn't like that, but the more Owen gave me glimpses into his world, the more intrigued I became. He led me down the path to submission, like the white rabbit leading Alice into Wonderland. Now, I'm hooked. I'm addicted to the pleasure only he can generate in me. I am his.

I am HIS.

Chapter One

I remember the first time with Owen taking control like it was yesterday. I was no stranger to Owen, his house, or even his body. We had fooled around countless times before, but this time would be the first I let him exclusively take the lead. We had discussed what I would like to try and the things he liked. He said he would work out the details and everything else that brought me here, standing on his doorstep, following his instructions.

I'm wearing the lacy sheer underwear and jersey maxi dress he insisted on. The stockings and the knee-high high-heeled boots are my own addition to the outfit. I take a deep breath, trying to calm down my accelerating heart, and I knock on the door.

Owen stands there in a t-shirt, jeans, and his feet bare, his eyes glistening as he looks me over before standing aside to let me in. When I step inside, he steps in behind me.

"Can I take your jacket?" he breathes at my neck while already pulling the denim from my shoulders. This simple act seems heightened by the situation. My skin tingles everywhere the denim brushes.

"Turn," he commands. "Let me look at you." I turn around on the spot for him, allowing him to take me in, letting his eyes roam over me. In a split second, he has me pinned against the wall in the hallway. His mouth descends over mine, and his tongue finds its way to mine, licking and caressing it as they roll over one another. His kiss is hungry and possessive, and his hands roam from my face down my body to my hips. He presses me harder against the wall before his hands settle around my wrists, trapping them.

He breaks our kiss and pulls my arms up over my head, pinning my hands to the wall above me. He shifts his hands so he's able to circle both my wrists in one hand, leaving the other free to caress over my body. It goes straight back to my hip, and he starts to crumple the material of my dress up, pulling the hem higher and higher until he can step back and look freely at what's underneath. When his eyes fall on my stockings and boots, they darken, and he holds my gaze with an unforgiving stare. Again, his lips collide with mine, more possessive than before, and his free hand goes to my lacy knickers.

He pulls back the waistband and slips his hand inside them until he's where he wants to be, directly between my legs. He uses his knee to force my legs apart. When he does, he pushes my legs out further, forcing me to move my feet, my legs wider, and his access is uninhibited. He wastes no time; his fingers move between my slick folds and he's inside me. I gasp against his mouth as his fingers drive deep, and he starts to fingerfuck me against his hallway wall.

The second my hips instinctively grind back against his touch, he breaks our kiss, pulls his fingers from me, and makes a great show of licking his slickened fingers, savouring the wetness like he's licking chocolate from his digits. He uses the hand that holds my wrists to pull me along behind him into his joined living room-dining room. He drags me in front of him, facing his dining room table. He pushes me forward, just a fraction, so my palms are resting on the tabletop. His knee again goes between my legs, and this time he forces me to spread my legs wider. My mind is racing with thoughts of what is to come. I bite my lower lip in expectation.

Owen's hands grab at my dress again, pulling it up, stopping only when it's bunched at my waist and my ass is exposed. He presses himself against my ass, and I feel the hard length of him through his jeans. He holds me firmly at the back of the neck and pushes my face to the cool surface of the tabletop. "You will *not* move," he commands, and my cheeks heat as I'm told what to do.

Owen's hand connects with my backside with a satisfying crack, and the initial sting settles into a burn that simmers through my ass, pussy, and clit.

"I didn't tell you to wear boots and stockings," he says as he smacks my arse again.

"No, Sir," I stammer, surprised at just how much being spanked is turning me on.

"I like them, so just this once I'll let you off with it. But don't think you'll be getting away with it ever again. Understood?" he asks as he continues to rain smacks on my buttocks.

"Yes, Sir."

Owen's hand strokes over my ass, and I hear his zipper being lowered. Before I know what's happening, he has yanked my underwear to the side and buried his cock deep into my pussy. He grabs my hips harshly and starts to pound into me without ceremony. "I don't like it when you don't do what you're told, girl," he warns as he thrusts hard and deep into my soaked sex.

There's something primal in the way he's taking me. Suddenly, I can see the appeal of submission all the more. I'm certainly enjoying the harsh fucking I'm getting, but I'm also feeling the need to atone for my indiscretion, to be back in his good favour, to allow him anything he needs for me to achieve that.

His fucking becomes more fervoured, and suddenly I realise this isn't about being fucked; this is about him taking what he wants, rushing to the finish line. He's using me as a means to an end, reinforcing my place within this little game of ours. My orgasm is only just starting to build and his is already about to wash over him. His fingers dig into my hips as he roars out in climax behind me, thrusting in as completely as he can before he spills his load deep inside me.

As soon as he's done, he withdraws from me and fixes my underwear back across my pussy. Sheer frustration washes over me. I'm so incredibly turned on, and I want nothing more than to climax, but I'm denied. Owen drops my dress back down over my backside.

He helps me get back up from the table and commands me to kneel in front of him. He holds his wet cock out in front of me. "Taste it," he commands. "Clean me up and see what you taste like."

I close my eyes and open my mouth, my lips surrounding his semi-erect dick. My taste buds are flooded with the flavour of my juices mixed with his, and I can't help but lick him greedily. I wouldn't have thought I would like to taste myself, but the frustration and the feeling of just how wet my pussy is against my knickers just adds to the sensation.

When he's satisfied with the job I've done and well on the way to being hard again, he leads me back over to the sofa and tells me to sit down. With every move, I can feel the juices leaking from my pussy and covering my underwear.

I see the slight grin pulling at the edges of his mouth. "Feeling good?" he asks me, clearly knowing too well how this feels. I shift in my seat and his grin spreads.

"Yes, Sir," I sigh.

"Have we learned a lesson now, girl? You're mine to use as I see fit. Even if that's using you to get myself off. You getting off is not a concern," he reminds me. Suddenly, I begin to wish I hadn't even mentioned the notion of orgasm denial. I'm beginning to see just how much knowledge he has on that very subject. I'm now sure of two very important things. One, Owen is not going to let me come today, and two, when he finally does allow it, I'm going to explode like a damn rocket.

For the rest of the day, Owen repeats the same process. He pulls my knickers to the side, fucks me hard, and spills into me. Then he straightens my underwear back up and carries on with the rest of my submissive experimentation. By the end of the day, my pussy is saturated with his cum and mine, and my lacy underwear is just as bad.

When the last 'game' of the day arrives, Owen strips me naked and ties me down over his dining room table. He tells me he's going to bury his cock in my ass, and that he's been looking forward to it all day. He tells me to open my mouth. When I do, my drenched knickers are shoved in as a gag and a tie tightened around my mouth to hold them in place.

When Owen pushes his cock into my ass, every frustrated nerve in my body is set on fire. As he fucks me slow and deep, a tsunami of pleasure takes hold of me. When I finally climax, it's so powerful that I'm sure all of the bones in my body have been removed and speech will never be possible again. That was the first time I ever knew what it was like to be someone else's. The first time I knew I would do anything to keep Owen happy if this was my reward. The first time he became *my* Master O.

Chapter Two

Sir was very vague in his instructions. He told me what to wear, where to be, but very little else. That's why I'm here in a deserted park at dusk, on a warm summer's evening, wearing a jersey maxi dress and white cotton underwear.

I do as I am told. I take a stroll around the outer path of the park, enjoying the last sunshine of the day. The cool breeze makes me feel aware of my skin. Anticipation of what is due to come has me wet, and the breeze stiffens my nipples and causes goose bumps to form on my skin.

I hear a twig snap behind me, and I turn to see if anyone is there. Finding no one, I turn again and continue on my walk. The sun finally starts to disappear, and shadows are forming around the picnic area as I pass. I feel like I'm being followed. Before I have the chance to turn and look, a hand is over my mouth and an arm is around my waist, lifting me off my feet and pulling me tight against the body behind me.

I feel his breath on my ear, and he whispers, "You need to keep quiet. If you don't, I know where you live. Understand, *little pet?*"

I swallow hard. It wasn't until the comment of 'little pet' that I realised what was happening, but the person behind me isn't Master O. At least, that's what I think.

I'm hoisted towards the shadows at the picnic area and pushed against a table in front of me, my 'attacker' behind me.

The hand at my waist moves to my hips and starts to pull up my dress. When he pulls me against him tightly, I can feel his hard cock against the small of my back. Cold metal slides against my hip and one side of my knickers gives way. I tense in his grip and attempt to scream, my heart racing at the thought of him brandishing a knife.

"Yeah, you feel that, don't you? You're going to do as you're told now, aren't you?" he breathes against my ear. I can hear the smile in his voice, and I shiver.

I feel him manoeuvring himself; the other side of my dress is also gathered up. The cold of the knife sends goose bumps over my skin as he cuts through the other side of my knickers and pulls them off in one move.

"Now, my little one, you're not going to move, are you?" he asks rhetorically as he grinds his hips against my back, brings his knife-holding hand to my mouth, and lifts the other just long enough to shove my balled up knickers into my mouth as a gag. He takes my hands, pulling them behind my back, and quickly restrains them there. I'm standing there in the middle of a darkened, deserted park, gagged, restrained, and with no panties on.

He pushes my legs further apart with his knees, his hands reaching up my body, cupping my breasts before groping and squeezing them roughly. He grabs at the top of my dress and yanks it down, exposing my white cotton bra. He roughly grabs at my breasts again, pulling on my nipples through the cotton before grabbing at the cups and pulling those down too, letting my breasts spill out over the top. He paws at me roughly, his hands kneading painfully into my flesh. I should cry out, but instead, I moan into the makeshift gag in my mouth.

"You're enjoying it aren't you, you little whore?" he chides me, breathing hotly across my ear. His unforgiving hands pull at my nipples, twisting them painfully. "You're going to take just what I give you, bitch, and you're going to like it, because all little sluts like a man to give them it hard, don't they?"

I whimper into the gag as he releases my hands and bends me over the table. My dress is once again lifted, this time exposing me to the cool evening air, my sex and ass now bare for anyone who cares to see. He kicks my feet, widening my stance again as he puts his hands on my bound wrists behind my back and pushes down on them. I'm flat against the bench, the still sun-warmed wood rough against my tender tits. He runs his hand along my slick pussy and plucks at my clit with his fingers, giving it a sharp squeeze. "Remember who you're dealing with, slut," he reminds me as I cry out into the knickers in my mouth.

His hand connects with my bare ass in a brutal wallop. The jolt carries me forward a little, rubbing my nipples against the jagged grain of the table. "Just for now, this is mine," he hisses at me in the encroaching darkness. "My ass, my pussy, my little whore, and I will do whatever the fuck I want with her." His fingers again run through my slick cunt, and he chuckles to himself. "All turned on and wet because she's getting fucked in the park for the world to see what a whore she is. Seems like I picked the right little pet," he mocks and thrusts two fingers deep into my soaked sex and begins fucking me roughly with them.

He withdraws them just as abruptly as he inserted

them, and again, his hand cracks down hard on my ass. The skin on my buttocks stings, sizzling right through to my clit. I shouldn't be enjoying this, but I am, and what's worse is he knows it. I hear his zipper, and a second later, I feel his skin against mine as he plunges his cock inside me. I cry out against his harsh penetration and his rough handling of me, but the gag in my mouth makes my sounds nothing more than a muffled moan.

"What's that, slut? You like my dick deep in your greedy little snatch? Mmmm, I think I agree with you on that one!" He gloats as he grabs my hair and pulls me upright against him. He rams into me with great force while he holds onto my breasts to keep us together. The harder he thrusts, the more his fingers dig into my flesh, grabbing me, bruising me as he squeezes my tits tightly.

He thrusts up hard and stops, pausing with me impaled on his cock, while he takes the time to cup my breasts more gently, pulling harshly on the nipples and twisting them cruelly. "Bet you're getting off on this, aren't you?" he whispers in my ear before biting my earlobe. I know that if this was real, I would be terrified, but he's right. I'm beyond turned on right now. I'm aching to have him thrust into me just a little bit harder, to pull on my breasts and nipples, and to have my screams of pleasure echo around this park. But I'm not the one in control here, and he's making that abundantly clear.

He moves his hands from my breasts to around my neck, holding me tight against him by the throat, my head tilted back as he bites into my shoulder. I cry into the knickers in my mouth, relishing the delicious pain he's inflicting on me. I try and move my hips to get the sweet climax I'm craving so badly, but he holds himself firm and keeps me pinned against him, forced to do the same.

"This isn't for you, dear," he sneers and pushes me forward. I lose my balance, and without my hands to save myself, I come down hard on the table, chest first, the rough wood biting into my skin. The harshness of the landing I receive is only intensified by the absence of his dick in my pussy. Before I know it, his hand is connecting with my ass cheeks again, over and over, reinforcing the point that this is not about my pleasure or me in anyway. This is a lesson in service, in taking what I am getting, regardless of what I want. Suddenly, Master O's keenness over my little rape fantasy is so very clear. I wanted the thrill of it, and he's teaching me that it's not about me. He's the one with the control; he's the one who understands my needs better than I do, that the submission is what helps me best deal with the situation.

When he's done smacking my ass, he rubs his hands over my scorched skin. I groan against my gag, on edge, needing to come, and not knowing what his next move will be. It isn't long before I find out. Fingers back in my wet pussy, rubbing everywhere, spreading my slickness around towards my ass. I tense; he couldn't possibly mean to fuck me in the ass like this, could he? His thumb teases over my asshole, and it's not long before I get my answer. The head of his cock pushes hard against my ass, demanding entrance.

He's not as lubricated as I'm used to, and there's a sharp sting as he pushes past the ring of muscle and forces his way into my ass until he is firmly embedded deep inside. I want him to take a minute to let me adjust, but I know it's not likely to happen when he starts to thrust into me, pushing ever deeper. When his balls press against my pussy, I know that's as far as he can physically go. I can't lie; it's not comfortable. It's not the vision I had in my mind when I told Sir about my darkest fantasies, but I also know I'm not so restrained that I can't just spit out my panties and scream my safe word if I want to. The thing is, I don't want to. I bite a little harder on the gag in my mouth when he withdraws almost completely to slam back into me. Soon enough, I'm moaning into my gag again, seeking that sweet sensation overload that only orgasm can bring me. But I can feel the cock buried in my ass begin to pulse. I know no matter what I want to achieve, he's about to get what he wants, and that's all that should matter to me. I hear him roar behind me, I feel him explode deep in my ass, and I wince at how hard he's gripping my hips to make sure he comes as deeply in my arse as he can.

My frustration is almost blinding, and I'm only vaguely aware of him pulling out of me. The next thing I know, my wrists are free, and as I slowly lift myself off the table on aching arms, he is nowhere to be seen. I pull my knickers from my mouth and look at the cut sides. I let the skirt of my dress fall back to my ankles, as it was when I first walked into the park. I adjust my bra and the top of my dress, recovering my breasts, making sure that if I bump into anyone, they would not be aware of what happened to me.

For a split second, I think about relieving my frustrations right there in the park. It wouldn't take long. I could hop on the tabletop, part my legs, let my dress ride up, and give myself the orgasm I so desperately crave. But that notion passes, replaced with slight guilt and a need to follow the rules of the scene that had unravelled before me. No matter what happens, I will not come by my own means.

Once steady on my feet and sure I'm at least outwardly suitable to finish my walk and get out of the park, I start towards the exit. As I pass by the gate, I see Master O's car and him inside. He beckons me over, and I approach.

"Get in," he commands. I open the door and slip into the seat beside him. "Nice walk?" He grins.

I nod, unable to put into words how I truly feel about the situation. Frustrated doesn't seem to cut it.

"Here..." he says, holding out a handful of items for me to take from him. "Put these in the glove box."

I look down, and in my hands, I see a knife and some cable ties.

"It was you?" I ask.

"Always, my sweet. You didn't think I would leave such an event to someone else, did you?"

I think about it for a second. Knowing how Sir handles things, honestly? No, I couldn't see him letting someone else experience with me what I just had.

"No, Sir," I agree with a sigh.

He glances over at me and grins as he starts the car. "Let's get you home. I think there's something I need to take care of for you." He smiles and leans over to my side of the car, placing his lips against mine, sliding his hand up under my dress and between my legs. He circles my clit, and the pent-up frustration has me exploding over his hand in mere moments.

He removes his fingers from under my dress, licking them as if they were the most delicious things he had ever tasted. "That will do, for now. At least until we get back to mine." He smirks, turns on the car headlights, and drives off into the twilight.

Chapter Three

Sir walks into the room with a bag in his hand and orders me to strip. I follow his commands quickly. I drop my jeans and panties to the floor before setting them on the armchair carefully, followed by my t-shirt and bra soon after. I stand there in the middle of Master O's living room completely naked, my head bowed, my chest out, and my arms flat by my sides. I stand with my feet shoulder-width apart, so my sex is always slightly exposed.

Sir opens his bag and produces his first gift for me. It's a collar, very similar to one a dog would have. He fastens a leash made from a metal chain and a leather wrist strap to the collar. Master O pulls on the leash, tugging me down, forcing me to move to my knees to prevent falling over. Once I'm on my knees, Master O tugs the leash again so I naturally fall forward onto all fours.

"Don't move," he commands, and I know I'll be remaining on my hands and knees for the rest of the session.

Sir returns to the bag again and produces two mitten-like gloves. It's not until he feeds my hand into one that I realise what they are. They are made from fur and leather and have been fashioned to look rather like paws.

Inside, they are designed to offer support to my wrists yet make my hands completely immobile and useless. He buckles each one tight. I know I wouldn't be able to get them off for myself, even if I wanted to.

Once my front paws have been secured firmly in place, Sir again returns to his bag. This time, he produces kneepads. He taps on my thigh, so I can lift my leg and allow him to fasten my kneepads in place. Once complete, I am left very comfortably on all fours.

Master O pulls on my leash, prompting me to turn with his tug as he manoeuvres me to a different position.

"You know what you are, don't you?" he asks.

I nod my head. "Yes, Sir," I reply.

"What are you?"

"Your dog, Sir."

"No." He laughs, "You're my bitch!"

I nod, accepting what is to come. "Yes, Sir."

Again, Master O dips into the bag he brought into the room. In his hand, he holds a strap with a strange piece of metal on it. It looks almost like a snaffle bit for a horse, but not quite. He tilts my head back and forces my mouth open with his thumb.

"Your tongue," he commands.

I stick my tongue out of my open mouth, and Sir slips the contraption over my tongue then pushes it all back into my mouth. The metal bracket naturally sits around the back of my bottom teeth and sandwiches my tongue between two further pieces, trapping it in such a way it's impossible to form any kind of words or speech. Instead, I can only groan or growl. Sir secures the device around my head tightly, and all speech is removed. I am purely his little dog. Indeed, I'm his bitch.

Sir returns to his bag once more and one final item is produced to complete my transformation. I face forward and stay completely still. I hear the little bottle in his hand flip open, and I wait to feel it. Cool gel tickles down between my buttocks to my asshole. Sir rubs the end of his last gift in the gel before pressing it against my arsehole firmly. I breathe deeply as he pushes against the tight muscles until suddenly, they give way. As a strange groan escapes my gagged mouth, my ass is filled with a fat plug. My ass tightens around the tapered part of the plug. Knowing it's now secure, I glance back over my shoulder, greeted by an extraordinary sight. Master O has given me a tail. It's long and looks like soft silicone, supple enough that every movement I make is translated into a wag of my tail by the soft rubber.

Sir rubs his hand over my back. "That's a good girl." He smiles. "Your name is now Ginger, and you're my little bitch. I expect you to be a good little dog. You will sit, stay, play fetch, go for walks, and if I need to, I will take you to the vet. Your food and water dishes are on the floor in the kitchen, and when you need the bathroom, you'd better scratch the door to be let out into the garden," he warns.

Heat creeps over my face at the humiliating thought of what he's just said.

"Now," he says, looking at his watch. "The vet should be here soon to check on my little bitch's health. Shall we play a game until then?" He grins.

A small sense of dread creeps over me. A vet? I don't get time to dwell on it any further, as Sir lifts a squeaky chew toy from his bag and squeezes it so it gets my attention.

He tosses it across the room, and I happily trot after it

on all fours before grabbing it with my limited mouth mobility and bringing it back to Master O. He pats my head and praises me. I can't help but feel a delighted warmth creep through me. I have pleased him, which in turn pleases me. Again, he squeezes my toy, making it squeak before throwing it and letting me trot after it again. Our game continues for a while, until the doorbell rings, and Sir lifts my leash and pulls me behind him as he goes to the door.

When he opens it, I see his friend, Thomas, standing there. Thomas shakes Sir's hand, glances at me, and says, "Is this the bitch you called me to the house about?"

Sir nods. "Thanks for doing a house call." He smiles and leads Thomas into the living room with me pulled along behind.

"Where do you want her?" Sir asks, and Thomas points to the dining room table.

"Up there should be good enough."

I'm pulled to the table, where Sir then lifts me and sets me on it, still on all fours.

Thomas pulls surgical gloves from his bag and puts them on. Then, out comes a stethoscope. He rubs the cold plate over my breasts before finally settling on the right position. He listens to my chest before nodding and putting it away again. He pulls my mouth open as much as he can around my strange gag and runs his gloved fingers over my trapped tongue.

A large syringe with no needle comes out of a box he has in his bag next.

"This will treat her for worms and fleas," he tells Sir before shoving the syringe to the back of my throat and emptying it. I recognise the taste instantly. This vet's 'medicine' is cum. "She'll need this regularly, Owen," Sir is told.

Thomas's hands rub over my whole body, as though he

really is inspecting me. His hands cup my dangling breasts and squeeze hard before pulling on the stiff little peaks of my nipples. His hands run down my back and over my buttocks. He pushes on the plug, which is held firmly in my ass. Without ceremony, two gloved fingers are shoved inside me, causing me to whimper.

"There, girl," Sir coos while stroking my head. "What do you think?" he asks.

"Oh, she's definitely good breeding stock," Thomas confirms. Sir grins at me, and I'm suddenly dreading what's going to happen next.

"Have you thought about having her microchipped?" Thomas asks.

I flinch; he can't possibly be serious. I shift around on the tabletop, but Sir yanks my leash hard and tells me to stay. He looks again at Thomas. "If she's as good a breeding bitch as you think she is, I guess I'd better," he announces.

I'm starting to panic. Thomas reaches into his bag again and pulls out a sealed pack, with a rather mean-looking syringe and a tag reader. I shift nervously on the tabletop.

"Hold her still!" Thomas demands.

Sir wraps his arm around my waist, facing towards my backside, and uses a tight bear grip to hold me still. Thomas smacks my right buttock before rubbing over it with a cold antiseptic wipe. I shift more, and Sir only uses more of his body weight to pin me into position. He leans into my body, immobilising me, and holding me tight against the tabletop, I feel the sharp sting of the large needle piercing my skin. It makes me cry out in an exaggerated whimper. There's a click and my buttock feels like it's on fire, then a cotton ball is held firmly against my skin where it has just been penetrated by the needle.

After a few minutes, Thomas discards the cotton and

grabs his chip reader. He waves it over my buttock, and it dings, making everyone present aware that it has found a microchip. I am branded forever as someone else's pet. Someone else's dog, for as long as the chip remains in my buttock.

My head spins, full of thoughts of what has been said and the implications of what has been done. Thomas packs up his bag, and I'm brought back to reality.

"She needs to be trained daily, Owen. If she's going to accept what she is, it's vital."

Sir nods. "Thanks, Thomas. I appreciate it."

Thomas nods too. "When she's ready, let me know," he says cryptically. Sir lifts me down from the table and walks Thomas to the door.

"See you again soon," Thomas says, shaking Sir's hand.

"Thanks again, Thomas. I'll be in touch."

Thomas pats my head. "You be a good little bitch. I'll be back."

Sir waves Thomas off and then closes the door. He takes me over to the corner to a large doggie bed. He pushes me into the bed and unclips my leash.

"Stay," he warns before patting my head. "Good girl, Ginger." He smiles before walking off.

I curl up as best as I can with a painful buttock. Soon, I doze off and dream of chasing a tennis ball across a deserted beach.

Chapter Four

I'm sitting in the corner of Master O's living room, in my usual position. I'm naked, my wrists and ankles have leather restraints, my nipples have clamps with little bells on them, and there's a collar around my neck. I sit with my bottom resting on my feet, my legs parted, and my palms flat on my thighs. I don't look at him, my eyes cast firmly to the floor.

Sir is moving around, setting things up, and I try not to let my mind run away with me over what he has planned for me this evening. He finally gets his spanking bench in a position he wants it in, and he looks at me and grins, catching me looking in his direction. I quickly avert my eyes again, knowing it's too late and I've been busted.

"I saw you, girl. But with what I have in store for you this evening, I think I'll let you get away with it, just this once." He grins, and as he does, the doorbell rings. Sir goes to the door, and I listen carefully to what is happening. Before I realise what's going on, I hear Sir asking whomever it is to come in. Panic sets in. My heart starts to race, and I feel my cheeks flush with colour, a hue that then seeps down my body. He's about to bring someone else into the house while I'm sitting here naked and ready to be used.

It's something Master O and I had talked about; the inclusion of other dominants in our playtime, but it wasn't something I was aware of him organising. I know when it was discussed, it was mentioned that it would be something I, aside from the use of my safe word, would have no control over. Once again, it's proven how much Master O listens to what I say, and just how much he plans to take all my fantasies and make them a reality.

The living room door opens, and Sir walks in, followed by two of his friends. I close my eyes and take a deep breath to silence the pounding of my heart in my ears. "Adam, James. This is Emma. She's my submissive little slut, and she's here for us to use this evening in any way we see fit," Sir announces to them, pointing in my direction.

One of Sir's friends claps his hands together in delight. "So, this is the little one you've been telling us so much about."

Sir puts his hand on his friend's shoulder. "Adam," he says, warning him. "Don't leer. It's not polite." He laughs.

My cheeks burn more, and my pussy clenches at what might be in store for me. I'm wet and ready, and yet so incredibly nervous about what might happen next. Adam, James, and Sir settle themselves on the sofa and Sir looks at me. "Girl, go and get our guests some drinks," he commands, and I quickly stand and walk to the kitchen. I get Sir's favourite drink, scotch on the rocks, for him and his guests. I come back in and hand over each drink. When I go to return to my space in the corner, Sir stops me.

"Kneel," he commands, and I sink to the floor in front of the three men. "Hands on your head," he orders, and again, I do as I'm told. He uses his foot to push my legs further apart before rubbing the toe of his boot into my crotch, pushing it into my wet pussy, and rubbing it along my clit a few times before dropping his foot back to the floor.

"Look at the state of my boot, you dirty little whore. You've got it all slicked up. Get down there and clean that up," he growls at me. I drop my hands from my head and nervously lean forward on all fours, extending my tongue out to lick my juices from the leather.

As I clean Sir's boot, a firm hand strikes my backside. A hand I know is not Sir's strokes over my warmed skin before being removed, and another smack connects with my upturned ass. "She's got a very spankable arse," Adam purrs and runs his finger along my sex. I try to keep focused on Sir's boot as Adam's finger strays between my labia and is pushed into my pussy in one move.

Adam begins to fuck me with his fingers as I keep licking Sir's boot. Sir pulls on my collar to lift me from the floor. He unzips his jeans and pulls me over his crotch. His hard cock springs free and he pushes my face down onto it. I feel someone moving behind me, and another set of hands roam over my body as Sir begins to fuck my face, while Adam's fingers plunder my pussy. James's hands reach around me and grope my breasts, and all my senses are on overload as I come over Adam's hand.

"I think she likes your fingers, Adam," Sir breathes, clearly liking what I'm doing as much as I'm liking what Adam is doing. Adam adds an extra digit and keeps thrusting in and out of my soaked sex. I can feel Sir twitch in my mouth. I run my tongue along the underside of his thick cock and am rewarded with a hot mouthful as he explodes. I suckle gently, licking everything from him, feeling my own climax building again.

My hair is grabbed, I'm pulled from Sir's cock, and my

face is pushed down on another. James fists his hands in my hair and thrusts his cock into my throat. I gag, and my eyes start to water. I glance up, begging him with my eyes to ease off, even a little. Instead. he grins and pushes me further. James moves to the sofa, using my hair to keep me tightly over his dick. I glance at Sir and see the lust shining in his eyes. He's enjoying me being used by other men, and something within me makes me want to keep him pleased and lustful. I force myself to breathe through my nose and take James's cock as deeply as I can.

Adam's fingers continue to thrust into my pussy, and another orgasm threatens to engulf me again. My head starts to swim between climaxing and attempting to control myself over James's cock. I feel myself letting go of the last bit of nerves, letting the physical pleasure and emotional satisfaction in pleasing my Master take over.

James pushes deep, stopping at the back of my throat at the same time Adam cracks his hand down on my ass. I jolt, and James is allowed to breach the barrier into my throat. I gag, and James's hold on my hair tightens. I feel Sir's hands on my skin, rubbing my back, encouraging me without words. I know by how his fingertips cover my skin that he's proud of me, that he's turned on by me, that I'm in control and free to give my safe word if I need to. I can *feel* it in every movement of his fingers on my sizzling flesh.

Tears roll over my cheeks, and as Sir's fingers finally roam over my nipples, I explode over Adam's fingers one more time, and James rewards me with a choking flood of hot cum down the back of my throat. He pulls his semi-erect cock from my mouth with a pop, and Adam lets his hand fall from my pussy. I am allowed to sit back on my heels, my heart pounding, my sex soaked, and my breathing erratic. When I glance at Sir, the look in his eyes settles me and he grins. His hand rubs over my shoulder, and I breathe deeply. I can feel him regarding me closely. I know he's taking in everything, analysing me, making sure I'm still okay with the situation I've found myself in at his insistence.

Master O takes my hand and leads me over to the spanking bench.

"Do it," he whispers in my ear. I don't need any further instruction than that. I stand to position myself over the bench, careful to line myself up as Sir has trained me to.

Once I've lowered myself into position, Sir circles me, locking me into place with a restraint on each limb. My thighs are held apart, my ankles also, my pussy and ass exposed. My arms are bound at the wrists, my tits falling through a conveniently positioned hole in the bench, allowing them to be freely accessed at any time.

Master O takes a blindfold from a table nearby and covers my eyes, plunging me into darkness, unable to see who is touching me, not knowing whose cock is being forced into me.

I take a breath before hands are on my breasts, pulling on my clamps, the attached little bells jingling with the constant manipulation. As I moan in pleasure at the sensation, a cock is pushed against my lips. I open wider and allow it to penetrate my mouth completely. It pushes back against my throat, and I try to breathe through my nose and fight my gag reflex. Its owner pushes hard into my throat before pulling back and thrusting back in just as hard.

I jump when I feel a cock at the entrance to my soaked pussy. I groan loudly as the cock enters me with a slow and steady pace until I'm completely impaled. The hard cock pushing deep inside me pulses before pulling back and ramming deep inside me once more.

I moan as my body starts to tremble with the overload of sensation: my body, pussy, and mouth filled, hands on my breasts and nipples, on my hips, digging into my flesh, a hand in my hair controlling me. I am being thoroughly used, and I'm on the brink of coming apart for the most fantastic orgasm of my life.

My stomach tightens, my pussy starts to pulse, and a cataclysmic climax rips through me. I cry out as my mouth and throat are filled with cum and lick greedily as the cock is pulled from between my lips.

The cock in my pussy is pulled out, and I hiss at the sensation. I hear movement around me before my mouth is presented with another cock. From the taste of it, the one that was deep in my cunt moments before.

"You're doing great, little one," I hear Sir saying somewhere near my rear. "Keep control while I spank you! No biting!"

Just as the cock touches the back of my throat, a paddle connects with my backside. Being blindfolded adds just enough of the element of surprise that I lose the focus needed to breathe through my nose. I gag on the cock in my mouth and my teeth graze it as it pulls back.

There's a hiss and a throaty lust-filled voice, "Dammit, O. Your pet's teeth are sharp!"

I can hear Sir chuckle behind me. "Don't worry, Adam. She'll pay for it later!" The dick is pulled from my mouth at the time an extra hard crack from the paddle connects again with my buttocks. A fiery sting burns through my skin invoking a yelp, and as I cry out, the hard cock is again pushed deep into my mouth.

The pattern of paddle and deep throating continues until I have lost all track of how many strikes my sensitive flesh has taken, and I'm left with only a deep sting in my ass with a burn that has spread to my pussy.

Sir's hand smooths over my ass cheeks, soothing me yet causing the skin to prickle with pain at the contact all the same. I feel the cool trickle over my ass as a digit spreads it over my tight asshole.

I groan as the digit presses into my ass, teasing me. The cock in my mouth pulses, and I hear Adam voice his appreciation. "Jesus, O. She liked that, and fuck, so did I!"

The digit is joined by another, and I moan around the cock again. It jumps in my mouth, and I know he's close. The fingers are slipped from my ass, and a cock is pushed against me in their place.

As the cock enters my ass, I buck against my restraints. I'm not in any pain, I'm on sensory overload. To Adam, with his cock in my mouth, it all proves too much, and I am rewarded with another mouthful of cum.

I swallow all I am given and lick the cock thoroughly before it slips from my mouth. I'm left with just the biting in my nipples from my clamps, my burning buttocks, and a filled and stretched asshole as Sir fucks me balls deep.

Another orgasm is quickly building within me. As I start to feel my ass twitching with an impending climax, hands grab my clamps and pull them from my nipples. There is a delicious burn of pain as the blood flows freely into them again. I scream out with abandon as my orgasm slams into me.

He holds my hips tightly and bucks his against me in a hard, unyielding pace. I'm not allowed to come down from my first orgasm this way as I'm caught by a second, and then a third in quick succession.

I'm vaguely aware of movement around me, but my euphoria won't allow my brain to focus on anything. A final orgasm approaches, and Master O explodes within me, roaring as he does, barely audible over my own screams of pleasure.

Moments pass and I am aware of the sensation of my back being stroked as I start to come back down. Sir slides his spent cock from my ass, and he disappears from my backside, his hands moving from limb to limb, releasing me.

He helps me back off the spanking bench to rest on my heels. I feel the slickness everywhere between my legs, my jaw aches, and my body is weak. His lips connect with mine in a slow and tender kiss.

"I'm so proud of you." I can hear him smile and he removes the blindfold from my eyes.

We are alone again in his house. There is no sign of the friends who had been here moments before. He stands, scoops me into his arms, and takes me upstairs to the bathroom. I am bathed, caressed, and cared for before being carried to Sir's king-size bed, where I fall instantly into a sated sleep in Owen's arms.

Chapter Five

It's been about a month since Master O made me his bitch, quite literally. I have spent hours every day being his little pet, playing fetch, barking at the postman, trotting around after him on my leash. The more I do, the more and more I slip into that delicious headspace where everything else falls away, and all I am and want to be is Ginger. I have made sufficient progress that I no longer have to wear my hateful tongue gag. I know my place and what's expected of me.

I'm lying in my doggie bed, just lazing and thinking about the new toy Sir bought me, when there's a knock on the back door. I lift my head and sit up, ready to bark. The door knocks again, and I stand on all fours and start to growl.

"Ginger!" Master O scolds.

I stop and trot after him towards the door to see who is invading my territory. When Sir opens the door, I see the vet standing there. I glare at him, and he starts to laugh.

"I see you remember me, Ginger," he says and pats my head. I clench my ass and feel my tail start to wag. "You might like me this time. I've brought you something to play with," he tells me before pulling on the leash I didn't realise he had in his hand, and another dog appears. I creep forward a little, sniffing the air around the other dog. It moves towards me, and I bark.

"Ginger!" Sir scolds again. "Be nice!" He grabs my collar and pulls me back from the door, allowing the vet and the other dog the space to come into the kitchen. Once the back door is shut, the vet unclips the other dog's leash and allows him to come towards me. I can't help but growl at the stranger in my house. The other dog bows his head and barks at me, and suddenly I think they might be okay. I might be able to let them play fetch with me or just generally run around with them.

I creep forward and sniff at them again. Sir offers the vet a coffee, while they watch us get to know each other. The other dog rubs his nose against mine, smelling me before taking a smell of my skin the whole way down my side. I follow his actions and smell along his skin. The other dog smells good; there is a scent that makes my skin prickle, and somehow, my pussy moistens. When I reach the dog's hip, I can see he's a large male. His nose reaches my back end, and I feel him pressing it against my pussy and can feel his breath on my skin. I nudge his hip with my nose and watch his tail wag. I run my own nose across his backside. The same sweet scent tickles my nose. I think this is definitely a dog I can play with.

I turn to walk off into the living room, and the vet's dog trots along after me. "This should work out well," I hear the vet telling Sir.

Sir agrees. "They seem to naturally be getting on well anyway." He looks at me. "Do you like Duke, Ginger?" he asks me, and I wag my tail and bark to show my approval.

Sir smiles and pats my head and Duke's and lifts my favourite toy before walking back to the door. I trot along behind him with Duke following me. Sir throws my tennis ball outside and I rush out after it, hoping to get to it before Duke. Duke bounds out after me and gets there faster, lifting my ball in his mouth and rushing back to the back door.

It's not until I turn around that I notice Sir has closed the door and left us in the backyard together. Duke drops my toy at the back doorstep and trots back over to me. He nudges my cheek with his nose, and I bark at him, bouncing on my front paws, ready to play. His tail wags and he jumps at me, knocking me onto my side. I roll on my back and use my front paws to pat at his chest. His paws are at either side of my head, and he nudges at my exposed chest, his teeth finding my peaked nipples as he playfully nips at my skin. I yelp, roll back to my paws, and growl at him before I bounce at him with my front paws, and he barks back. I bounce again and Duke falls over. I waste no time in putting my mouth to his neck, nipping at his skin, letting him know who is alpha.

"GINGER!" Comes the scold from the back door. I look up to see the vet shouting at me. I release Duke and trot to the door, leaving him to get up and follow me. "Get in!" the vet scolds.

I trot into the house and Duke comes with me. Sir clips my leash back on my collar and pulls me into the living room behind him. He settles himself on the sofa and pulls on my leash before putting it under his foot, so I'm stuck and can't move.

The vet comes in after Sir and moves behind me. He has a little jar in his hand. He opens it before dipping a finger into it and then smearing it over my entrance. A heat starts to burn into me.

"Duke!" the vet calls, and his dog trots in on his command. Sir unclips my leash again, and I involuntarily wriggle at the feeling spreading through my sex.

Duke trots over behind me, and the vet nudges him in the direction of my backside. I feel Duke's nose at my ass, and his tongue licks a long, wet stroke over my sex. I yelp and turn away from him. When I do, I can see that whatever the vet put on me has Duke excited, his thick hard cock bobbing between his legs.

I'm startled by the sight and again move away from him, but Duke follows me, clearly attracted by whatever coats my backside. Again, his nose nudges against my ass, and his tongue takes another long lick of my sex. I'm soaked and inexplicably turned on, as though whatever balm has been applied is purely there to set my nerves on fire.

Duke takes delight in repeatedly rubbing his tongue in long strokes over my sex. I want to move, but the desire is taking over; I want more of his tongue instead. I stay still and let him work my soaked sex into more of a fury. I fidget and open my hind legs to allow Duke better access, and a whimper escapes from my mouth.

Before I know it, Duke's on my back, his cock bobbing against my pussy. I'm suddenly painfully aware of what's going on. I remember the vet's words on his first visit about me being a breeding bitch, and fear takes over. I move, causing Duke to stumble off my back. Everything in me wants to get up and move away from Duke on two legs. But I glance at Sir and see the look on his face and the bulge in his jeans; I know that this is what he wants, this is something that would please him.

Torn between what to do next—move away from Duke

or satisfy something Sir wants—I freeze. Duke takes that as his cue to mount me again. His skin is warm, and his chest covers my back. Again, his cock bobs at my entrance. He licks my shoulder and bites into my flesh as I flinch against him. My hind legs open a touch wider again, and he pushes his hips against me. The first time, his cock finds my pussy but slips past. The second time, however, Duke's cock sinks into my pussy, and he begins to buck against me, his dick thrusting back and forth into me. His hold on my shoulder causes a pain that seems to make my clit sizzle more. It's not long before I'm panting, on the edge of orgasm. Duke continues to pound into me, hard and frantic. I clench and pulse around him as my climax surges through me. Duke starts to growl, and his cock pulses and explodes inside me. The second he's done, Duke pulls out of me and lets his cock and cum slip from my slit. His nose returns to my pussy as he licks the length of me again, lapping at his own juices mixed with my own.

The vet and Duke stay at Sir's house the rest of the day. I lose count of the number of times Duke takes me. But by the end of the day, I'm actively encouraging him, nudging his ass with my nose before running my tongue over his balls, seeking him out to mount me and fuck me.

As they leave, Sir pats my head. "You did well today, Ginger," he praises. "It looks like you're not just my bitch anymore, though. Looks like you're Duke's bitch too." He grins at me. Knowing this pleases him pleases me. I walk tenderly back over to my bed in the dining room, settling down, my pussy still filled with Duke and very sensitive from the bout of rutting that was done to me. Again, I doze off, this time dreaming of the next time I might be able to see Duke.

Chapter Six

It's been about eight months since I started playing with Owen and experimenting in the BDSM lifestyle. We have played a lot, and our relationship both as Dominant and submissive has changed, as has our friendship. He told me he felt that he wants to test me. Apparently, he thinks it's something I'm ready for. It thrills me and makes me nervous all at the same time. I want so much to please him, but at the same time, I worry he's picking something that's going to push me too far.

I take a deep breath and knock on Owen's door. He smiles sweetly when he sees me.

"Come in, little one." He grins and kisses me softly. 'Don't worry, I have faith in you," he tells me, reading me perfectly without me having to say a single word to him. That element of our relationship is new to me, to have someone capable of understanding me so completely, to read me, to be inside my head and see my thoughts and fears so clearly. It's a strangely comforting experience now that I'm over the initial unnerving feeling it gave me.

Master O ushers me into his living room, where he has

the spanking bench set up and ready for me. He smiles at me and rubs his fingers along my arms.

"Strip," he commands and places a kiss on my neck.

I follow his command without hesitation and stand with my hands by my sides. His hands roam over my skin.

"You know I want to test you, don't you, little one?" he asks.

"Yes, Sir," I reply softly.

"You know that all you have to do is say your safe word, don't you, pet?"

I nod. "Yes, Sir."

He smiles and puts a finger under my chin to tilt my head towards him. "Good," he whispers against my lips before kissing me tenderly.

He takes my hand and leads me to the spanking bench. I drape myself over it as I have done countless times before, and Sir circles me, securing me tightly to the bench. He strokes his hand down my back before spanking my ass hard. I flinch with a groan at the contact. Sir comes back round towards my head and gathers my hair in his hand, pulling my head up. With his free hand, he unbuttons and unzips his jeans and frees his stiffening cock, pressing it at my lips.

I open my mouth and allow him to slide his cock across my tongue, and I close my lips around him and suck. Sir grows harder in my mouth and starts to thrust into my throat. His firm hand in my hair and his forcefulness in taking my mouth make me wet, and I show him with the enthusiasm with which I flick my tongue over his shaft. Sir uses my mouth as he needs to, moaning as his cock starts to pulse in my mouth, and his hips buck against my face with a little less control. My eagerness is rewarded when Master O explodes down my throat with a loud groan.

Sir stoops to lick the taste of himself from my lips with a kiss. I moan against his mouth, turned on by his demands of me this far. He moves to my rear, and I am quickly rewarded with his tongue lapping at my wet labia. He nuzzles his face against me before his tongue swirls over my clit. The situation has me so primed; it isn't long before that delicious feeling starts to brew low in my belly. When Sir's tongue swirls around my asshole, I cry out as a climax hits me. His finger continues to work my clit as his tongue sweeps over my ass, and his teeth suddenly sink into my buttock as he bites me hard.

A second orgasm takes over me as Sir plunges two of his long fingers into my soaked pussy, his thumb still circling my clit.

"I love how wet you get for me, my little slut," he teases against my buttocks as he curls his fingers inside me. He's been slipping more and more verbal humiliation into our play, and I have to admit it's been more of a turn-on than I ever thought possible. I love hearing him call me names. I moan as he rubs over my G-spot and continues to taunt me. His free hand strokes over my back and reaches for my nipples and breasts through the gap in the spanking bench, and again, I climax over his hand.

I'm aware of how he's working me a lot, and it makes me a little apprehensive about what he has coming. That nervousness mixed with his actions makes me wetter, my head spinning with possibilities. He brings me out of my thoughts with a firm twist of my nipple.

"You're ready for it, aren't you, my little slut?" he asks.

I have no idea what he's asking me if I'm ready for, but I know whatever it is, I want it, and I want it now. He pulls his hand from my pussy, and I groan out in frustration.

"I'm going to push you, my little pet. I'm going to test

you, and if you pass, then I might just have a reward for you," he tells me. I look up at him and want nothing more than to prove to him that I am ready for whatever test he has. Whatever he wants to push me with, I will accept his challenge.

"Please, Sir," I say, and I can see from his grin that he is happy with my reaction. He pulls a blindfold from his pocket and places it over my eyes, kissing my cheek as he does.

"Good girl," he whispers against my ear, and I shiver at the sensation it raises in me. His hands are again on my breasts, groping them roughly and pulling on my nipples. Suddenly, I feel the nip of nipple clamps, but ones I have only had a few times. These have teeth; mean little crocodile clips that bite into my tender flesh. I wriggle against my restraints, every inch of my body suddenly super sensitive to any stimuli. I feel Sir at my ass and wonder what is coming next.

"You're not gagged. If you need to use your word, do so," he reminds me before landing a paddle against my ass. I jump at the unexpected jolt, and my pussy clenches at the thought of him paddling me repeatedly, more than he ever has before, wondering if that is to be my test. He continues to strike my ass, over and over, at least ten times before stopping. A vibrator is placed against my clit, and I am teased. My body responds to his attention on my clit, and I start to shiver with another impending orgasm. As I approach that point, the vibrator disappears, and the paddle returns to connect with my buttocks.

Master O repeats this pattern over and over. Pushing me to the brink of orgasm, only to force me back down with the paddling of my ass. I have no idea how long he has been doing this because my frustration has taken over, and I just want to come. He paddles me again and tears start to fall from my eyes. I'm so desperate for release that I can't take it anymore.

Sir stops paddling my backside and strokes over my enflamed skin. My ass is burning, and so are my pussy and clit. Needy, wanton, and every single touch from him just makes me worse. He pushes something cold and wet against my asshole, and I assume it's a plug coming. Sir slowly pushes the plug into my backside, and I groan, needing more. My ass is smacked again, and I clench around the new plug. Suddenly I'm aware of a new sensation. My asshole is starting to tingle and burn.

"Can you feel that?" Sir asks, and I can hear his smile.

"Yes, Sir!" I reply breathlessly.

"That's a finger of ginger, my dirty little girl. It's going to burn for about twenty minutes or so, and I'm going to enjoy torturing you even more while it's there. If you clench, you'll make it worse on yourself. Understand?" he asks.

I nod. "Yes, Sir." I try not to clench the ginger root finger that's buried in my ass; every time I do, I feel the extra burn. Sir's fingers are in my wet slit, and he pushes something against my clit.

"That's ginger too, slut. You're going to like how it makes you feel," he tells me, and with that, his contact with me disappears.

The constant tingle in my ass grows into a burn. My clit is tingling, and I can't help but want to wriggle, needing more. I clench in need and the burn intensifies instantly. I cry out with a groan, and I hear a chuckle nearby. A second later there is a pull on my nipples. I'm vaguely aware of what he's done, he's clipped weights on the clamps on my tits. I groan more. I need to come; my frustrations are at a fever pitch. I feel desperate like never before for an orgasm, to be fucked, to climax. I am beyond needy.

I hear another chuckle and feel Sir whisper near my ear, "That's the ginger, little slut. It makes you a wanton little whore. You'll be begging me to fuck you by the time I'm done with you."

Another slow, agonised groan escapes from me, and I'm compensated with a spank on the backside. Again, I clench my ass involuntarily at the contact, which elicits an intense burn that borders on painful for my actions. The feelings are intense. It's overwhelming and overpowering, and I almost want to scream out and beg for him to free me and fuck me every way he can, but I don't want to give in. I don't want to let myself down, never mind Master O.

I have no idea how much time passes, but Sir mixes the stimulation between the paddling of my backside, the pulling on my nipples, and the constant presence of the ginger in my ass and on my clit. My mind is spinning; I can't focus on a single thought. I've regressed to a moaning little whore with only one blinding need; to be fucked hard and to come. It's a need so great that it's practically painful. The burning in my backside is subsiding, and I don't know if it's because it's naturally wearing off or because everything else is so overriding it pales in comparison.

Sir fists my hair in his hand, and his cock is pressed against my lips. He pushes it hard, forcing it back towards my throat. "Is this what you want?" he gloats over me before fucking my face hard for several minutes.

I choke and nod as he pulls out of my mouth. "Yes, Sir!" I gasp, and my mouth is filled with his dick once again.

"Beg for it," he commands me this time as he pulls it from my face again.

"Please, Sir. *Please!* I *need* to come. I want your cock," I whine, my mouth filled with cock again the second I pause. He thrusts between my lips, hitting the back of my throat each time. He's teasing me more. It's what I want, but it's not where I need it the most. I moan over his length and wriggle in my restraints. The movement sets the weights swaying on my nipples, stimulating me further. He yanks himself from my mouth with a pop, tugging hard on my hair.

"Stay still!" he warns.

"*Please,* Sir," I beg. I don't care anymore; I need it. I need to feel him deep in my pussy.

Master O moves away from me, releasing my hair. He unclips the weights on my nipples, leaving them still clamped. He moves behind me, flicks the ginger from my clit, and then slowly pulls the ginger plug from my ass. I groan. As much as it caused an unpleasant sensation, the removal of the only thing that was filling me leaves me feeling bereft. His hands land on my backside, and his thumbs pull my labia apart, exposing me further. Seconds later, his cock is thrusting deep inside me in one single stroke.

I cry out as Sir sets a punishing pace, fucking me hard, his fingers digging into my hips as he drives into me over and over, racing me to the edge of a cliff, ready to jump off into a tidal wave of orgasmic bliss. I feel it starting; the pull in my lower stomach, the tingling in my clit, and just as I think I'm about to shatter into a million pieces, Sir withdraws from my body and smacks my arse hard.

I whimper, and tears fall from my cheeks. I can't take it anymore. I want to come; I need to more than I need to even breathe at this very moment. Sir moves in front of me and pulls my blindfold off. I look up at him and I'm overwhelmed by the look on his face. His eyes are swimming with lust, but he looks genuinely tender and caring; pride and love shine from his face as he looks at me and his hand goes into his pocket.

"I want to do something else. Do you trust me?" he asks.

I answer without a second of hesitation, "Yes, I trust you, Sir." He smiles and removes his hand from his pocket. He shows me what he has. It's a collar with a little metal plate riveted on it. 'Property of Master O' is engraved on the plate. A small padlock goes with it. I smile up at him and nod. He slips the collar around my neck and locks the padlock. He pulls a small dog tag-style necklace from the collar of his t-shirt and shows me the key for the padlock.

"We can sort a less obvious one for when we're not in scene. But I want you, little one. I want to keep you as mine, look after you, challenge you. To watch you grow in your submission," he explains.

I smile broadly up at him. We had talked about the concept, but never in terms of it happening between us. Who would have known you could want something so much, despite having given it no thought before?

"Now you can have what you want." He grins, moving behind me again and thrusting back into my pussy in one movement.

I groan. Warmth floods me, not only from the orgasm that's quickly building within me again, but because Owen, the man and the master, wants me around, to care for me, to nurture my submission, to do what he is doing right now, driving me to an earth-shattering orgasm. The world around me disappears as my climax crashes into me, made even more intense by the knowledge that I am his... I am owned.

THE END

* * *

Enjoy this? Why not read the next in the series - Seduced

The One-Handed Reads Series is made to do exactly what you might think!

Katriona craves control in all things. Her job. Her relationships. Her sex life.

One fateful night in a bar, she meets Mike. Confident, charismatic, cheeky, and not at all submissive. But there's just something about him that Kat can't resist.

Now she finds herself with someone determined to challenge her at every turn. Can Kat maintain the upper hand, or will she be seduced by the brat who is breaking every rule she has?

About the Author

Dee Lish is an Irish author who loves to indulge her imagination with some filthy stories. She's been publishing under other pen names since 2014, but in 2023 returned to her erotic roots.

She likes to spend what little spare time she has binge watching her favourite shows, reading, and making messes and memories with her two children.

You can follow her on social media, or join her newsletter for all the latest naughtiness!

Also by Dee Lish

Succumb to Me Series

The Mistress

The Ponygirl

The Handled

The Punished

The Corrupted

The Student

One Handed Reads Series

Teased

Owned

Seduced

Tempted

Desired

Unexpected

* * *

Dee Lish also writes romance as Leighann Duncan

www.authorleighannduncan.co.uk

www.ingramcontent.com/pod-product-compliance
Lightning Source LLC
Chambersburg PA
CBHW030812190726
48285CB00003B/1138